# *Gray Squirrel at Pacific Avenue*

*To my mother — Evelyn Cynthia Spolane.*
— G.H.

*For David, Matthew, Chandler,*
*Jo, Denny and all the other wild critters I love.*
— M.C.R.

10 9 8 7 6 5 4 3
Printed in Singapore

*Acknowledgements:*
   Our very special thanks to Dr. Charles Handley of the Department of Vertebrate Zoology at
the Smithsonian's National Museum of Natural History for his curatorial review.

*Library of Congress Cataloging-in-Publication Data*

Harrington, Geri.

Gray Squirrel at Pacific Avenue / by Geri Harrington ;
illustrated by Michele Chopin Roosevelt.
         p.        cm.
Summary: Gray Squirrel has a busy day hunting for seeds and nuts while avoiding the
neighborhood predators.
         ISBN 1-56899-115-0
[1. Squirrels — Fiction.]  I. Roosevelt, Michele Chopin, ill. II. Title.
         PZ7.H2375Gr 1995                                          94-27521
         [E] — dc20                                                CIP
                                                                   AC

# Gray Squirrel at Pacific Avenue

by Geri Harrington

*Illustrated by Michele Chopin Roosevelt*

Soundprints
*Where Children Discover...*

The October sun pours into the small backyard of the pink house on Pacific Avenue. A furry head pokes out of a nest of small leafy branches high in the live oak tree. Gray Squirrel has just woken up.

He scurries out to a branch and startles a kinglet, which flies away.

Scratching his ear with his hind foot, Gray Squirrel watches white-crowned sparrows feasting on birdseed at the feeder below. A scrubjay screeches from a manzanita bush, nibbling its dark red berries. Gray Squirrel is hungry too!

He leaps through the tree crown like an acrobat. The branches bob under his feet. He hears the familiar bark of the brown dog that lives behind the fence in the yard next door. Gray Squirrel rushes to the ground, spiraling down the trunk head first.

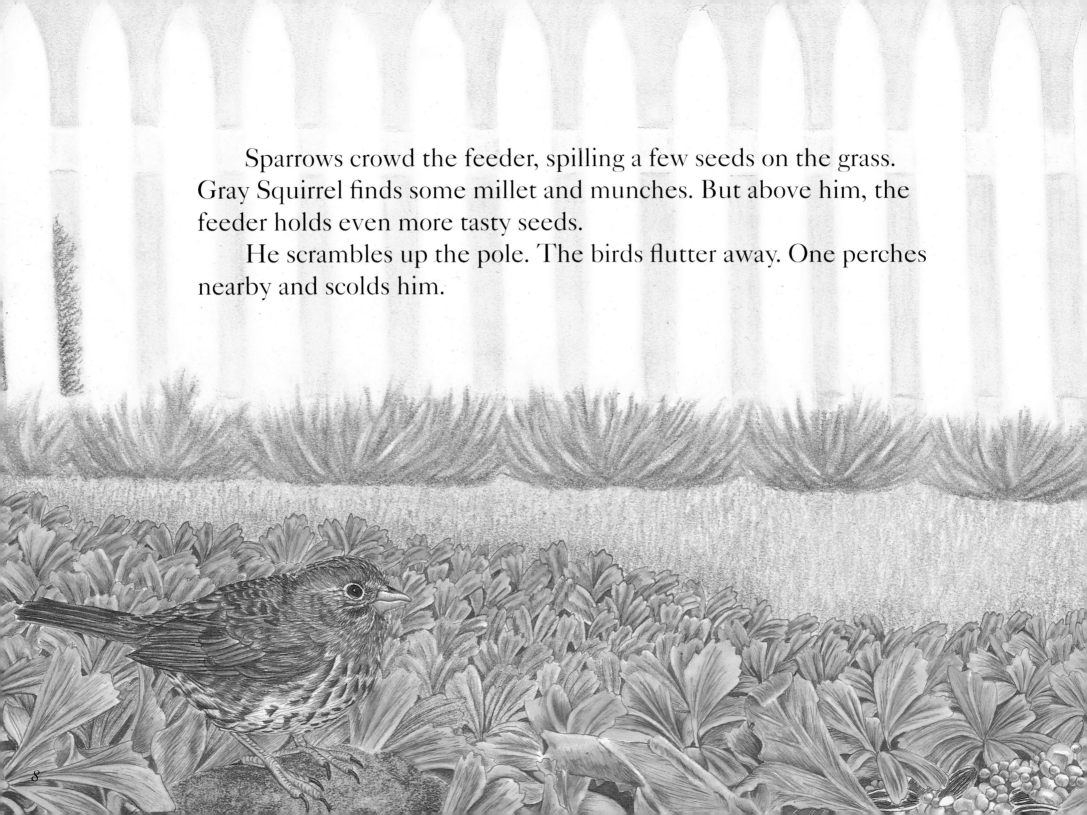

Sparrows crowd the feeder, spilling a few seeds on the grass. Gray Squirrel finds some millet and munches. But above him, the feeder holds even more tasty seeds.

He scrambles up the pole. The birds flutter away. One perches nearby and scolds him.

Gray Squirrel dips his pointed nose in the birdseed and eats, scattering the seed hulls. Too close to the perch's edge, he suddenly slips and loses his footing! He hangs onto the edge of the feeder with one paw. Dangling, he manages to reach with his other paw and pull himself back up.

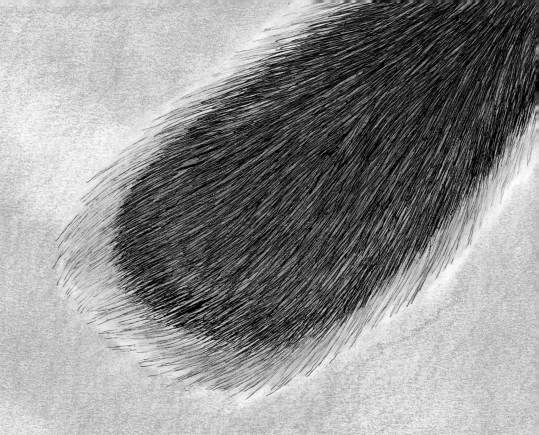

With his keen eyes, he checks the backyard for predators. The yard looks empty. Gray Squirrel jumps to the ground. But he has made a mistake!

He comes nose to nose with an orange cat, who is hiding under the manzanita bush. The cat's tail twitches. Gray Squirrel bounds toward the oak. The cat springs, but just as he does, Gray Squirrel leaps high onto the trunk.

The cat sprints up the tree, but Gray Squirrel is gone. He has rocketed from a branch, landing on the fence five feet away. Into the next yard he dives.

With quick breaths, Gray Squirrel darts across the strange lawn.

"*Grrrr...*" Behind him the snarling brown dog stands ready to attack.

The dog charges, but Gray Squirrel springs up an apricot tree. He hurries through the branches and vaults over the dog's head onto the fence. Along the fence-top he runs, finally leaping back to the oak in his yard.

17

All this scurrying has made Gray Squirrel hungry. He hears a chipmunk rummaging for acorns in the dry leaves below. The cat is nowhere to be seen. Gray Squirrel scoots down the oak and chases the chipmunk away. From behind a rock the chipmunk chitters at him crossly.

Gray Squirrel snatches a shiny brown acorn in his paws. With sharp front teeth, he cuts the hard shell in half and devours the nut inside. After finishing five more acorns, he digs a little hole in the ground, drops in another acorn, and covers it with earth. He will save this nut for later.

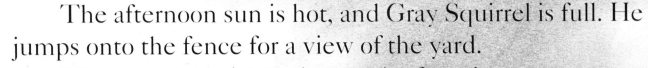

The afternoon sun is hot, and Gray Squirrel is full. He jumps onto the fence for a view of the yard.

The orange cat is nowhere to be found.

Next door the brown dog has fallen asleep.

Pigeons nibble politely at the fallen seeds.

Gray Squirrel raises his tail over his head for shade.

Then he licks his front paws and washes his nose and ears. He combs his fur with his teeth and claws.

The backyard is at peace.

*"Screeech!"* The screen door flies open, and the pigeons scatter. Out of the house bounds the orange cat.

On the fence-top Gray Squirrel freezes. His enemy spots him and pricks up his ears. He leaps onto the fence, ready for some fun.

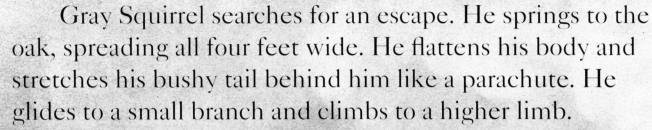

Gray Squirrel searches for an escape. He springs to the oak, spreading all four feet wide. He flattens his body and stretches his bushy tail behind him like a parachute. He glides to a small branch and climbs to a higher limb.

The cat jumps to the base of the tree, watching. Gray Squirrel fluffs his tail, holds it straight up behind him and quickly flicks it.

"*Tchuck! Tchuck!*" He stamps his hind feet.

The orange cat crouches to spring up the tree.

"*RUFF! RUFF!*" The brown dog suddenly charges through a loose board he has discovered in the fence.

The cat hisses. The dog growls. They whisk around the base of the tree until the cat makes a dash to the front yard. The dog follows close behind.

Gray Squirrel watches calmly from his lofty limb.

He takes a deep breath. Finding a comfortable spot,
Gray Squirrel relaxes, spreading his body out on the branch
with his tail draped over his back. Then, he closes his eyes
for a peaceful rest high in the live oak tree in the backyard
of the pink house on Pacific Avenue.

## About the Gray Squirrel

Gray squirrels live throughout the eastern United States and have been introduced on the west coast. They are found in forests, parks and backyards where food is plentiful. With a diet consisting primarily of seeds, nuts, fruit and insects, gray squirrels often store food for times of shortage by burying nuts in the ground. They locate them again through a highly developed sense of smell.

Appropriately named, gray squirrels have fur that blends with the gray bark of the trees in which they live, helping to protect them from predators. Their large, bushy tails are used for balance, to signal other animals and for warmth in a winter nest.

Best known as an acrobat, gray squirrels can leap up to four feet from the ground to a tree trunk. They can run along the top or bottom of branches and can even hang by their hind feet. When they jump long distances, up to twelve feet from tree to tree, they spread their bodies out with their tails flattened for balance.

## Glossary

*acorn:* A nut with a hard, shiny, brown shell that grows on an oak tree.

*chipmunk:* A small, striped ground squirrel that makes its home in a den beneath the ground.

*crown:* The leafy upper part of a tree.

*hulls:* The outer shells of seeds.

*live oak:* A tree with leaves that stay green all year round.

*manzanita bush:* An evergreen shrub with small, red apple-like fruit that grows in western North America.

*millet:* A cereal grain eaten by birds, animals and people.

*predators:* Animals that hunt and eat other animals.

## Points of Interest in this Book

*pp. 6-7* scrubjay, house finch (red-headed bird).

*pp. 6-7, 10-11* white-crowned sparrows.

*pp. 8-9* fox sparrow.

*pp. 18-19, 20-21* chipmunk.

*pp. 20-21, 28-29* ivy.

*pp. 22-23* pigeons.